Oink! Moo!
How Do You Do?

Oink! Moo!

How Do You Do?

A Book of Animal Sounds

by Grace Maccarone
Illustrated by Hans Wilhelm

SCHOLASTIC INC.

Cartwheel
·B·O·O·K·S·®
New York Toronto London Auckland Sydney

To B.G.F.
— *G.M.*

ISBN 0-439-05965-8

12 11 10 9 8 7 6 5 4 3 2   9/9 0/0 01 02 03 04

Printed in the U.S.A.   08
First Scholastic paperback printing, February 1999

Oink! Moo!

How do you do?

Baa! Hee-haw!

Come see what we saw!

Ribbit! Tweet!

There's lots to eat.

Hoot! Meow!

Let's hurry there now!

Honk! Neigh!

We're on our way!

Cock-a-doodle-doo!

I'm coming, too!

Caw! Cluck-cluck!

We're in luck!

Gobble-gobble! Ruff!

We've had enough.

Scat! Shoo!

Away with you!

Squeak! Quack-quack!

It's good to be back.

Chirp! Buzz!

What a great day it was!

Cheep! Cheep! Cheep!

And now to sleep.